TOFFEE
the Highland Cow

Marghanita Hughes

Scottish Children's Press

First published in 2002

by

Scottish Children's Press

Unit 13d, Newbattle Abbey Business Annexe,
Newbattle Road, Dalkeith, EH22 3LJ
Tel: 0131 660 4757 • Fax: 0131 660 6414
e-mail: info@scottishbooks.com

www.scottishbooks.com

text and illustrations copyright © Marghanita Hughes, 2002

the right of Marghanita Hughes to be identified as the Author
of this Work has been asserted by her in accordance with the
Copyright, Designs and Patents Act, 1988

BRITISH LIBRARY CATALOGUING IN PUBLICATION DATA
A catalogue record for this book is available from the British Library

ISBN 1 899827 51 X

Printed and bound in Scotland
(Bell & Bain Ltd *and* Bookbinding by Crawford)

Toffee Goes Camping

Marghanita
Hughes

For Mum and Dad

Try and find me on every page!

Toffee was **SO** excited, she'd never been on holiday before.

'Are we nearly there yet, Mum?' Toffee asked.
'No, but it's just a few minutes more.
Look! You can see the loch now.'
'Here we are!' shouted Farmer George.

Toffee followed her mum through a little wood full of really **tall** fir trees.

Suddenly, two red furry animals whizzed past her and disappeared up a tree.

'They looked in a hurry,' said Toffee.
'What are they, Mum?'
'They were red squirrels and they were probably fighting over some nuts.'

They came to a clearing and Toffee could see
the loch spread out before her. 'Wow!'

Toffee thought it looked like
a huge puddle – the biggest she'd ever seen.

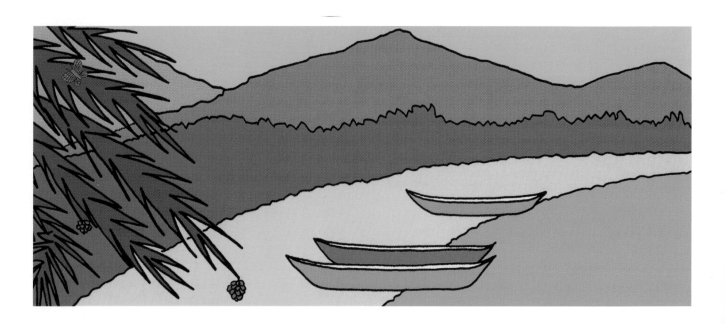

There was lots of yellow stuff as well.
As Toffee walked on it, she felt herself sliding a little.
'It feels funny,' thought Toffee,
'it tickles and gets stuck in my feet.'
'This is called sand,' said her mum.

Toffee had fun making a sandcastle.

Later, Toffee decided to explore a little. Mum had
fallen asleep under a tree, next to the beach.
Toffee liked the hot sand tickling her feet.

As she walked around the loch, she heard a loud

SPLASH!

Toffee looked up to see a brown, shiny-looking creature.
'Hello!' said the otter, 'I'm Ollie.'

'Hello!' said Toffee, pleased to meet a new friend.
'I've got something to show you,' said Ollie,
diving under the water. In a minute she was back,
pushing something with her nose.

'What's this, Ollie?'
asked Toffee.

'It's a canoe – jump in!' said Ollie.
It was a little wobbly but Toffee soon got the
hang of the oars and followed Ollie to her home.

Ollie lived on the loch bank. Her home was in an old tree. It looked very dark inside but Toffee thought it was great, nice and cosy.

'MY home is far away on the farm. I wish I could show you,' said Toffee. Then she remembered something. 'Come with me,' said Toffee.

'Here's where I'm sleeping tonight,' said Toffee
as she showed Ollie the tent. 'I'm camping.'

The next day Toffee decided to go up the mountain. Up and up she walked, higher and higher and higher.

As she climbed through the heather, out popped a capercaillie.

'Watch where you're putting your feet,' said the grouchy capercaillie.

'Oh, I'm sorry,' said Toffee. 'I didn't mean to hurt you, this heather is really hard to walk through.'

In a little while she had reached the top.

'What a view!' thought Toffee. She could see all around her. Everything, even the big loch, looked really small.

It all seemed very far away and Toffee felt afraid. She was lost.

As a light mist began to settle, she sat down and began to cry.

'Don't cry,' said a soft voice.

'Who are you?' sniffed Toffee, lifting her shaggy head.
'I'm Dandelion,' said the deer. 'What's wrong?'

'I'm lost and I can't get back down,' said Toffee.
'Don't worry, I'll help you,' said Dandelion. 'Follow me.'
Dandelion leaped through the heather and
Toffee plodded behind him, being careful not to
stand on any capercaillies or grouse.

Once they'd reached the bottom, Toffee felt much better and she asked Dandelion if he'd like to play for a while.

They played leapfrog at the edge of the loch.

What fun they had!

Back at the tent, they found Ollie.
'I've had quite enough adventure for one day,' said Toffee
as she crawled into the tent.
'Zip it up quickly, before the midgies get in,' giggled Ollie.

The next day, Toffee and her mum had to
go back home to the farm.

Toffee was sad to leave her new friends but
she promised to come back.

'Bye, bye, Ollie!'

she shouted as Farmer George
started the engine.

'Bye, bye, Dandelion!'

But Toffee doesn't have to wait until next year,
she can still see her friends in her dreams.

Endangered Animals

Capercaillie – this bird lives among the fir trees on hills and mountains. They are very difficult to spot.

Midge – like a mosquito and just as irritating! The males often dance in large swarms.

Mountain ringlet – this butterfly is fond of heather and it only flies when the sun shines!

Otter – a large carnivore of the weasel family. River pollution and hunting has made it rare to see an otter.

Red Squirrel – due to an epidemic disease, the red squirrel has declined in numbers (the grey squirrel having invaded their feeding places). Red squirrels are very shy but can be found in their favourite tree, the conifer.

Toffee is always having adventures!

Find out what happens when she goes
for a walk on her farm . . .

TOFFEE

At Home on the Farm
MARGHANITA HUGHES

also published by

Scottish Children's Press

ISBN: 1 899827 50 1

Visit **TOFFEE** at www.highlandtoffee.com
and
www.scottishbooks.com